Please help the Moonglow [...]

Our brave and loyal friend, Arrow, has travelled far from our world to protect the magic key that keeps our kingdom safe from the dark rabbits. Arrow is very far from home and will need your help.

Could you be his friend?

This magic bunny might be hard to spot as he is very small and often appears in different fluffy bunny disguises – but you can recognize him by the rainbow twinkle in his eyes.

Thank you for your help!

Strike
Leader of Moonglow Meadow

Sue Bentley's books for children often include animals, fairies and magic. She lives in Northampton in a house surrounded by a hedge so she can pretend she's in the middle of the countryside. She loves reading and going to the cinema, and writes while watching the birds on the feeders outside her window and eating chocolate. Sue was brought up surrounded by small animals and loved them all – especially her gentle pet rabbits whose fur smelled so sweetly of rain and grass.

Sue Bentley

Classroom Capers

Illustrated by Angela Swan

PUFFIN

To Tinka Minka — handsome lion-headed little bunny

PUFFIN BOOKS

Published by the Penguin Group
Penguin Books Ltd, 80 Strand, London WC2R 0RL, England
Penguin Group (USA) Inc., 375 Hudson Street, New York, New York 10014, USA
Penguin Group (Canada), 90 Eglinton Avenue East, Suite 700, Toronto, Ontario, Canada M4P 2Y3
(a division of Pearson Penguin Canada Inc.)
Penguin Ireland, 25 St Stephen's Green, Dublin 2, Ireland (a division of Penguin Books Ltd)
Penguin Group (Australia), 250 Camberwell Road, Camberwell, Victoria 3124, Australia
(a division of Pearson Australia Group Pty Ltd)
Penguin Books India Pvt Ltd, 11 Community Centre, Panchsheel Park, New Delhi – 110 017, India
Penguin Group (NZ), 67 Apollo Drive, Rosedale, North Shore 0632, New Zealand
(a division of Pearson New Zealand Ltd)
Penguin Books (South Africa) (Pty) Ltd, 24 Sturdee Avenue, Rosebank,
Johannesburg 2196, South Africa

Penguin Books Ltd, Registered Offices: 80 Strand, London WC2R 0RL, England

puffinbooks.com

First published 2010
1

Text copyright © Sue Bentley, 2010
Illustrations copyright © Angela Swan, 2010
All rights reserved

The moral right of the author and illustrator has been asserted

Set in Bembo
Made and printed in England by Clays Ltd, St Ives plc

British Library Cataloguing in Publication Data
A CIP catalogue record for this book is available from the British Library

ISBN: 978-0-141-33244-4

www.greenpenguin.co.uk

Penguin Books is committed to a sustainable future
for our business, our readers and our planet.
The book in your hands is made from paper
certified by the Forest Stewardship Council.

Prologue

Arrow hopped across Moonglow Meadow. His strong paws kicked up dust from the dry patchy ground. Nearby there was a muddy puddle that had once been a sparkling pool. The spring that fed it was a mere trickle.

He had returned just in time!

The tiny gold key he wore on the chain round his neck glowed brightly and a cloud of crystal dust appeared. It floated down and a fresh carpet of grass and wild flowers sprang up, spreading out over the whole meadow, and the spring began flowing again.

Arrow watched as his fellow magic rabbits began emerging from their burrows. Some hopped over to the pool to drink and others began hungrily eating the new fresh grass.

A large older rabbit with a wise expression and a dark-grey muzzle bounded towards Arrow.

'Strike!' Arrow bowed his head in greeting before the leader of the warren.

'Greetings, keeper of our magic key,' Strike said warmly in a deep velvety voice. 'Because of you, Moonglow Meadow is lush and green again.'

Arrow felt a glow of pride at the leader's praise. As the chosen guardian of the magic key, it was his responsibility to keep it safe.

'Have the dark rabbits agreed to come and live with us?' he asked the leader, hopefully. The deep gully next to Moonglow Meadow was home to a neighbouring warren of dark rabbits. Their land had become so dry that nothing grew there any more and they were hungry.

Strike shook his head regretfully. 'No. They still refuse to share our land.'

'But how will they survive without our help?' Arrow asked.

The leader's eyes darkened with anger. 'By stealing our key. They want to use it to make their gully green and beautiful again!'

'But without the key's power, Moonglow Meadow will become a desert,' Arrow gasped, his silver-tipped ears flattening nervously.

'That is why you must go to the Otherworld. Hide there with the key, so the dark rabbits cannot find it.'

Arrow felt very frightened of all the unknown dangers he must face, but he took a deep gulp and raised his head. 'I will do it!'

Strike gave a soft but piercing cry.

All the rabbits hopped towards Arrow and Strike and formed a circle around them. Suddenly the golden key around Arrow's neck glowed so brightly that for a moment he couldn't see.

The light slowly faded and where the pure white-and-silver magic rabbit had been now stood a tiny fluffy silver-blue bunny with huge chocolate-brown eyes that twinkled with tiny rainbows.

'Go now! Use this disguise,' Strike said. 'Come back only when Moonglow Meadow needs more of the key's magic. And beware of dark rabbits. They will try to find you.'

Arrow lifted his tiny fluffy chin. 'I will!'

Thud. Thud. Thud. The rabbits began thumping their feet in time. Arrow felt the magic building and a cloud of crystal dust shimmered around him as Moonglow Meadow began to fade . . .

Chapter
ONE

'Come on, Wolverines!' Julia Hill called
happily. She tucked a strand of her
wavy blonde hair behind one ear as she
marched across the lumpy uneven grass.
'We'll get team points for putting the tent
up by ourselves!'

Julia took a big breath of fresh air.
A patchwork of fields, hedges and trees
stretched into the distance, where they

met the hills. She could see the cotton-wool shapes of sheep on the gentle slopes. It seemed a world away from the busy town where she lived.

She had been looking forward to the school camping trip for ages. It was the first time she'd be spending a whole week away from her parents. She felt quite grown-up at the idea of taking care of herself.

Five of Julia's classmates from Blakestone Primary School followed her. One of them was lagging behind. Julia wasn't surprised to see it was Ellie. She was small and pretty, with glittery pink slides in her shoulder-length blonde hair.

'Wait for me!' Ellie called, gingerly picking her way between small mounds of sheep droppings.

Julia sighed as she waited for Ellie to catch up. When their teacher had sorted them into teams, she had been worried that Ellie might not enjoy the trip. She usually sat on the benches at playtime, while Julia and her best friend, Lucy, played ball games and tag. Lucy was on a family holiday and hadn't been able to come camping with the rest of their friends. Julia felt a pang of sadness as she thought about the fun they could be having together.

Julia could see the other teams had already picked their camping sites. The Bears, Elks and Cougars all seemed to be getting on well with putting up their tents. One of the boys looked over at the Julia and the Wolverines.

'The Bears rule!' he called, punching the air.

Julia's eyes sparkled. 'Not if we can help it!'

'We'll get our tent up first,' a boy standing next to Julia said confidently. 'I've been camping with my parents heaps of times.'

Lex was one of the oldest boys in Julia's class. Julia didn't know him all that well as he'd only joined the school mid-term.

'Great!' she said to him, glad that someone in their team knew what they were doing. Maybe this trip would be a good time to get to know Lex better.

'Let's go!' Lex's blue eyes gleamed. He spread his arms like an aeroplane and zoomed down to where the field narrowed and sloped slightly towards a hedge. Off to one side, there was a stile that led to a footpath.

Julia and the others followed.

Lex stopped near the bottom of the field. 'Here's a good place for our tent. We'll have it all to ourselves.'

'This looks perfect!' Julia was dumping her backpack on the grass when there was wail from just behind her as Ellie skidded to a messy halt.

'Oh, yuck! That's *so* gross!' she

complained, frantically wiping her designer pink trainers on the grass. 'I hate smelly sheep and I hate this messy field. Why couldn't we have stayed on a nice neat caravan site?'

'Duh! Camping equals tents. Get it?' Lex rolled his eyes. As Ellie fished a crumpled tissue out of her shorts pocket and dabbed at her pongy trainer, he started laughing. 'Ellie Darlow, nil – sheep poo, one!'

Ellie went bright red. 'Oh, shut up!' she muttered, doing a one-legged shuffle down the slope.

'Why do we have to have *her* on our team? She's going to be useless,' Lex grumbled loudly.

'She'll be OK.' Julia thought Lex was being a little hard on Ellie, who obviously wasn't as keen on camping as she was. Although she did hope that Ellie would start enjoying being in the outdoors soon – she knew that Lucy would have loved every minute. 'So, what do we do now?'

'You lot unpack the tent and lay everything out on the ground. And I'll stand here and tell you how to put it up,' Lex said bossily.

Ellie frowned. 'Who made you team leader?'

'I was joking, you muppet!' Lex undid the tent pack and upended it, so everything fell out on to the grass.

Julia ignored their squabbling. She picked up the page of printed instructions that lay on the grass and began to read them.

'We won't need those. I know what

I'm doing.' Lex grabbed the crumpled
tent. But after a few minutes of studying
it from all angles, he gave a snort of
disgust. 'I've never seen one like this
before. The stupid thing's faulty.'

'It's not the tent that's faulty,' Ellie
muttered.

'Hang on. I think I've worked it
out,' Julia said hurriedly, peering at the
diagram with the instructions. 'Look, the
poles and everything are all attached to

the inside. They're jointed and folded up like an umbrella.'

The other team members stepped forward to help Julia. With a few twists and a bit of jiggling, the jumble of fabric and tubing was transformed into a bright-blue dome shape.

Lex quickly took over. 'Those dangling bits of stringy stuff are the guy ropes. They keep the tent upright and stop it blowing away in bad weather.' Lex showed the others how to fasten the ropes to the ground with tent pegs and then stood back. 'Ta dah!'

'It looks a bit wonky on one side,' Julia observed. Half of the tent seemed to be sitting in a dip in the ground. 'Maybe we should move –'

'Oh, let's just get inside,' Ellie

interrupted, combing her hair with her fingers. 'I need to shake out my clothes. My jeans must be horribly creased.'

'Oo-ooh, so are mine!' Lex said in a silly babyish voice. 'I think I might ask Mr Potter to iron them for me.'

The others laughed. Ellie narrowed her eyes and glared at him.

Julia hid a smile. Lex and Ellie were like a double-act. She hoped they weren't going to argue all holiday, though. Not for the first time that day, Julia found herself wishing that Lucy had been able to come on their trip. Lucy was great at stopping arguments and Julia was certain that she would have found a way for everyone to get along.

She felt a couple of raindrops plop on to her head. One of the boys felt them too and there was a sudden mad scramble to get into the tent. Julia forgot about the tent being lopsided as she crawled in after the others.

There was a bit of jostling and scuffling about as everyone tried to decide on the best place to sleep. In the end, just for the sake of peace, Julia spread her sleeping bag nearest the porch opening.

Rain began drumming on the tent in earnest. *Oh great*, Julia thought. She needed to go to the loo and the toilet block was back at the farmyard.

Ellie was unrolling her sleeping bag. It was violet with little flowers all over it and had a matching pillow. 'Right, everyone. Now we need to check for spiders,' she announced.

'There can't be any in here. The tent's

only been up for about five minutes!' Lex said.

'Says you! If I wake up with a big leggy brute on my pillow, I'll scream the place down!' Ellie promised.

'Don't be so pathetic –' Lex began.

'I hate spiders too!' One of the other girls stuck up for Ellie.

Julia didn't mind spiders. The poor things were scared of people, and she often rescued any she found in the house and put them outside. A row looked like it might break out, so Julia pulled on her hooded waterproof jacket and crawled out of the tent.

'I won't be long,' she called, but no one answered.

From outside the tent, Lex and Ellie could still be heard having a go at each other. Julia sighed, starting to feel a bit fed up with them both. She agreed that Ellie could be a bit fussy at times, but Lex wasn't helping by being so bossy. If only Lucy were here – she knew she'd laugh with her at how silly Lex and Ellie were being.

Black clouds had gathered overhead and there was no one outside. The other teams were all sheltering inside their tents too. The grey stone buildings of Penryth House looked washed-out behind a curtain of lashing rain. Julia jogged towards the farmyard.

She reached the toilet block and shook out her wet jacket before going into a cubicle. After washing and drying her hands, she went and stood in the doorway that opened on to the yard.

It was still raining heavily and Julia was wondering whether to run straight back to the tent or wait for the rain to ease off. Suddenly there was a flash of bright light and a shower of crystal dust drifted towards her like a shimmering cloud.

'Oh!' Julia blinked hard, trying to make

sense of what she was seeing. As the dust slowly dissolved, she spotted a tiny fluffy silver-blue bunny crouching in the rain.

'Can you help me, please?' it asked in a small scared voice.

Chapter
TWO

Julia stared at the cute fluffy bunny in utter amazement. The pattering of the heavy rain on the metal roof had sounded almost like a tiny voice for a moment. She shook her head slowly. This might be the first time she'd been around farm animals, but she was pretty sure they couldn't talk!

She saw that the bunny's long floppy

ears were laid flat and it was twitching its silver-blue nose nervously.

The poor little thing was getting soaked. Where had it come from?

Julia hoped it wouldn't run away as she moved towards it, but it didn't seem too scared of her, despite its tiny size. She bent down and gently picked it up and then dashed back into the shelter of the doorway.

'Got you! Don't be scared. I won't hurt you,' she crooned softly. She felt the bunny's little heart fluttering against her hands beneath its wet fur.

'Aren't you gorgeous?' She held the bunny against her T-shirt to warm its tiny wet body. 'You must belong to someone who lives here.' But the tiny bunny had very unusual colouring, quite different

friend

from the wild rabbits her teacher had
pointed out when they arrived.

'I do not belong to anyone.' The
bunny's voice trembled and it gave a
shiver.

Julia's jaw fell open and she only just stopped herself from dropping the little bunny in shock. She looked down at its fluffy silver-blue fur. Bits of it were sticking up in little wet spikes.

'You . . . you really can talk! How come?'

'All of my warren can talk,' the bunny told her, looking up at her proudly. 'I am Arrow, of Moonglow Meadow. May I ask your name?'

'I'm Julia. Julia Hill. I'm here at Penryth House Farm with the rest of my class from Blakestone Primary. We're . . . um . . . on a camping trip,' she said, still having trouble taking in a talking rabbit.

Arrow dipped his head in a formal bow. The effect was slightly spoiled by the tuft of damp silver-blue fur sticking up between his ears.

'I am honoured to meet you, Julia.'

'Me too.' Julia nodded awkwardly, trying to keep a straight face. Arrow was the cutest thing she had ever seen, especially with his spiky hairstyle. 'Is Moonglow Meadow part of this farm?' she asked.

'No.' Arrow shook his head. 'It is very far away in another world.'

Julia heard something tinkle softly and saw that Arrow wore a fine gold chain round his neck with a key hanging from it.

Arrow noticed her looking at it. 'I am guardian of this key, which keeps our meadow lush and green. But our neighbours, who are fierce dark rabbits, want to steal it. Their land is dry and stony and they are hungry, but they refuse to share our meadow. They want to take this key to make their own land lush and green again. If they do this, Moonglow Meadow will become a desert.'

'Oh no! That would be terrible!' Julia exclaimed.

'Yes. That is why I have come to this world to hide and keep the key safe.'

'That must be really scary for a tiny bunny like you,' Julia said gently.

'Please put me down, Julia,' Arrow said. Rainbows gleamed brightly in his warm chocolate-brown eyes.

Julia bent down and put him on the floor.

'Stand back,' Arrow ordered. As he rose up on to his back legs and his key began flashing, Julia felt a strange warm prickling sensation down her back.

A cloud of shimmering crystal dust appeared and swirled around Arrow. When it cleared, Julia saw that the cute fluffy silver-blue bunny had gone. In its place stood the most magnificent and impressive rabbit she had ever seen. It was as big as a large cat and had silky white fur, flecked with silver. The tips of its large upright ears looked as if they'd been dipped into molten silver.

Julia gasped, completely spellbound.

'Arrow?' she gulped in wonderment.

'Yes, it is still me,' he told her in a smooth velvety voice.

Before Julia could get used to seeing him in his true from, there was a final flash of light from his key and Arrow reappeared as the tiny silver-blue bunny.

'Wow! That's a brilliant disguise!'
Arrow's little bobtail twitched
nervously. 'Yes. But it will not fool the
dark rabbits if they get too close. I must
find a place to hide. Can you help
me, Julia?'

'Of course I will!' Julia said without thinking. She wanted to protect this brave little bunny, who was here, all by himself, in a strange scary world. 'I'll have to smuggle you into our tent, so the teachers don't get suspicious. Just wait until the rest of my team see you!'

'No, Julia. I am sorry, but my mission is secret. You can tell no one about me. Promise me?' the magic bunny asked anxiously.

Julia felt disappointed. She'd been hoping that having a magic bunny around would make Lex and Ellie forget about their differences and get along with each other. But she wanted to do everything she could to keep Arrow safe.

'OK then. Your secret's safe with me,' she said. 'But it's going to be really difficult to keep you hidden in a small tent with six kids inside.'

Arrow pricked up his ears. 'I will use my magic, so that only you will be able to see or hear me.'

'You can make yourself invisible? Cool! That makes things much easier,' Julia said with delight.

The magic bunny's key flashed. 'It is done.'

Julia scooped him up again, cuddled him against her chest and then drew her waterproof jacket closed around him. 'There! Nice and cosy,' she announced.

She pulled up her hood and stepped out into the rain, which was starting to ease off. Arrow's fluffy little body was warm as he snuggled up to her. She felt her spirits lifting as she tramped down the

wet field towards the tent.

Although she still wished Lucy were
here, it would be a lot easier to cope with
Lex and Ellie squabbling now that she
had her own secret magic bunny friend
for company!

Chapter
THREE

'Rise and shine, teams!' Miss Granger's cheery voice came from just outside the tent. 'Meeting in the farmhouse common room to sort out chores and activities before breakfast. See you all in fifteen minutes sharp!'

There were a few grunts and yawns inside the Wolverines' tent as everyone poked their heads out of sleeping bags.

'OK, miss!' Julia called sleepily.

There was something soft and fluffy curled up near her left shoulder. She put her hand up to feel it and it moved.

'Arrow!' she burst out delightedly. The girl sleeping opposite gave her an odd look, and Julia quickly pretended to have a sneezing fit. 'Atchoo!'

She must be more careful about keeping her magic bunny a secret.

'Did you sleep well?' Julia whispered to Arrow when the girl looked away and she'd made sure that no one else was looking.

Arrow touched her chin with the tip of his little damp nose. 'Very well, thank you. This is a safe place. I like sleeping in a tent with you, Julia.'

'Good! Because I love having you

for my friend!' She kissed the top of his warm little head. 'I s'pose we'd better get up.'

Julia had been lying on her side with her knees bent. As she stretched, she thrust her legs down into the sleeping bag and gasped as her bare feet met cold, soggy material. The bottom of her sleeping bag was soaking wet.

Gently moving Arrow aside, she got out, crawled forward and unzipped the curved opening into the porch. A big puddle covered one side of it. It must have gathered there overnight, after all the heavy rain. Julia was nearest the tent's entrance, so it had seeped towards her sleeping space.

'Look at this. I said the tent was wonky!' she said crossly. 'We should have moved it.'

'You never said anything about it being wonky,' Lex said.

'Yes, I did!' Julia retorted. 'But you and Ellie were arguing and no one was listening to me. And then it started raining –'

'So the rain is my fault, is it?' Lex butted in huffily.

'No, but –'

'Don't blame me either,' Ellie said,

twisting a strand of her blonde hair between her fingers. 'Everyone seems to be picking on me at the moment.'

'I'm not! I didn't mean . . . Oh, just forget it, OK!' Julia said, exasperated. Turning away, she struggled into the dry clothes that she had folded beneath her pillow last night. 'Those two want to turn everything into an argument,' she whispered to Arrow.

Arrow nodded. He jumped up on to a rolled up sleeping bag at the back of the tent, out of harm's way while everyone was moving about inside the small space.

'I don't believe it!' a boy complained, as he crawled into the porch and picked up his bag. 'My clothes are completely soaked.'

'So are mine!' a girl said. 'I can't wear

any of them. Someone should have
listened to Julia about the tent . . .'

'Look. You can both borrow one of
my T-shirts,' Julia said quickly, as Lex
frowned and opened his mouth to speak.
She didn't want *another* row to break out.
'And someone's probably got some spare
jeans that'll fit you. I don't mind staying
back here and hanging all the wet clothes
up to dry, while you go to breakfast. I'll
see you all there,' she said, for the sake of
keeping the peace. Besides, she wouldn't
be alone. She had Arrow with her.

'Are you sure you don't want any help?' Ellie asked.

Julia shook her head. 'No. I'll be fine. Honestly.'

There were nods and murmurs from her other team-mates. A few minutes later, the Wolverines went out, leaving Julia alone with Arrow.

'Phew!' she said, relieved.

Now she could talk to Arrow without having to worry about anyone hearing. The magic bunny hopped over and jumped into her lap. Julia gave him a quick cuddle.

'I'd better try to get my sleeping bag dry. I don't fancy cold wet feet tonight,' she said, wrinkling her nose. Arrow hopped out of the tent behind her, as she dragged her sleeping bag outside and draped it over a nearby bush.

'There's not enough room for all the wet clothes. If we had an old-fashioned clothes airer like Gran's, I could put the other kids' stuff on that,' she said, thoughtfully.

Arrow's whiskers twitched curiously. 'What does this airer look like?'

'It's a bit like three small ladders, joined together at the sides so they stand up. Like this.' She drew an 'N' shape in the air with her hands.

'I understand.' Arrow's golden key flashed.

Julia felt a warm tingling sensation down her spine as a cloud of crystal dust appeared and drifted away towards a wood near the bottom of the field. Almost immediately a bundle of sturdy

twigs dropped out of thin air on to the
grass in front of her.

Snap! The twigs trimmed themselves
and formed into the shape of ladders.
Creak! Green vines bound them together.
Rustle! The airer marched across the
grass like a soldier on parade and stood to
attention.

Julia clapped her hands in delight.
'That's brilliant! Thanks, Arrow.'

'You are welcome.'

She ducked back into the tent to sort out the wet clothes. It didn't take very long to hang them out to dry. 'I just hope it doesn't rain again.' Julia bent down to pick up Arrow. She stroked his warm ears. 'Let's go after the others, before someone comes to see where we are!'

But it was too late.

'What are you still doing here, Julia?' asked a stern voice.

Julia almost jumped out of her skin. She'd been so busy that she hadn't heard anyone approaching. She turned to see Mr Potter, the strictest teacher in school, looking at her over the top of his glasses.

Chapter
FOUR

'Um . . . I was just trying to . . . erm . . .
dry out some of our things,' Julia said.

'Hmm.' Mr Potter walked over to the
wet clothes draped on their twiggy dryer.
'This is a clever idea. You should get
team points — although I can't believe
that you made it all by yourself,' he said
suspiciously, peering down to examine it.
His eyebrows knitted together in a frown.

'Did someone who works at the farm
help you?'

Julia gulped. If Mr Potter thought she
was cheating he'd probably punish her by
making her peel mountains of potatoes,
or worse!

'It was . . . erm . . . a team effort,' she improvised quickly. 'All the Wolverines helped. I . . . um . . . volunteered to stay behind to finish hanging the clothes out to dry. They got wet because we had a big puddle in the tent.'

Mr Potter nodded slowly.

Julia held her breath, hoping that he'd believe her. After a moment, the teacher's stern face softened.

'Well, I must say, the Wolverines have done very well,' he said. 'Top points for initiative. Come along now, Julia. You don't want to miss breakfast.'

He strode back towards the farm. Julia quickly tucked Arrow beneath one arm, before hurrying after him. She bit back a grin as she looked down at her magic bunny.

'I'd better explain about the airer to the team, before they speak to Mr Potter,' she whispered. Somehow she didn't think there would be any arguments from anyone, even Ellie and Lex, about them getting extra team points!

Arrow's big soft-brown eyes gleamed.

'Mmm. Delicious!' Julia finished eating the enormous breakfast of sausages, beans, eggs and toast. It had been cooked by the teachers and a couple of farm workers, but from now on all the teams were going to take it in turns to cook meals.

Arrow was in her lap, munching a small piece of toast.

'I thought you'd never been camping before,' Lex said. 'So how come you knew how to make that clothes dryer thing?'

Julia grinned at him. 'I'm just a natural genius!' she joked. 'So, who's any good at washing dishes?'

'Not me. I'm rubbish,' Lex said, jumping to his feet. 'Gotta go. I've . . . erm . . . forgotten something.'

'No you don't!' Ellie grabbed his arm. 'Wolverines have to do kitchen chores today. That means *all* of us!'

'Haven't they ever heard of dishwashers here?' Lex grumbled.

'If we all do it, it won't take long,' Julia said, agreeing with Ellie for once. Maybe there was hope that they might all work together as team. Ellie seemed a lot less sulky and spoiled today.

Lex seemed about to answer back when Mr Potter gave him a stern look and he slunk towards the washing-up area instead.

Julia felt Arrow jump down on to the
floor. He sat under the table as she stood
up and began collecting plates and cutlery.
She was drying cups on a tea towel
when he whooshed over in a rainbow
of sparkling dust and landed on a nearby
window sill.

'The whole camp's going on a hike
down to the beach when we've finished,'
she whispered to him. 'I'll have to collect

my backpack first. You'll be safer inside it.'

After Julia had finished drying up, she went back to the tent and found her bag. With Arrow tucked safely inside it, Julia and the Wolverines joined the other teams and trooped across the fields of grazing sheep. Mr Potter strode ahead, swinging a large black umbrella that he used like a walking stick.

The sun broke through the clouds as they emerged on to the beach path. The ground sloped gently downwards and Julia had her first glimpse of the sea.

Arrow was sitting up to look out of her bag. His nose twitched. 'I smell something strange. It smells like salty water.'

'That's the sea,' Julia whispered. 'Look, you can see it over there.' She pointed towards the huge expanse of blue that met the sky at the horizon.

Arrow pricked his ears. 'It looks very big,' he said nervously.

'The sea *is* big. But you won't get wet if you stay on the beach. That's what the wide strip of sand in front of the sea is called,' she explained.

Arrow stretched up even further out of
the bag as Julia and the others walked on
to the beach. The sea breeze stirred his
fur and blew Julia's blonde wavy hair into
her eyes. She took a stretchy hairband out
of her jeans pocket and gathered her hair
into a ponytail.

'Right, everyone,' Mr Potter said. 'Have

a good time, and keep an eye out for shells. Lots of them get washed up on this coast. Your team task is to collect as many different kinds of shell as you can.'

'Bor—ring,' Lex murmured.

'I love collecting shells. They're so pretty,' Ellie said.

'You collect them then. I'm off to have a paddle!' Lex plonked himself on the sand and started pulling off his shoes and socks.

For the second time that day, Julia agreed with Ellie. She loved looking for shells too. She was just about to suggest that they look for some together when Ellie squealed. Lex had dropped a bit of seaweed down her back and was laughing as Ellie tried to fish it out of her T-shirt. Julia rolled her eyes – why could her team not get along?

'I'm going to walk up the beach. See you later,' Julia called to the other Wolverines.

Arrow leaned out of the bag to peer down at the sand, his nose twitching with curiosity. 'I would like to look more closely at this strange stuff. What is it made of?'

Julia trudged through the deep soft sand. 'Crushed shells and rocks, I think. You might have trouble hopping across it. It's better down there.' She pointed towards the damp, firmly packed sand nearer the shore.

Arrow jumped down and began nosing about. He was nibbling at a tiny piece of seaweed when he uncovered a slimy piece of crab shell. He jumped backwards, sneezing and snorting in disgust.

'Oh, poor you! I picked one of those up once. They smell awful!' Julia said, sympathetically. She took a water bottle out of her bag and poured some water into her hand for him to drink.

Arrow lapped at it gratefully. 'Thank you, Julia. That is better.'

They walked on and Julia picked up a dozen different shells, which she put in her backpack. She didn't know what they all were, but she recognized the long razor clams and dark-blue mussels.

'I could use my magic to help you find some special shells,' Arrow offered.

'Thanks. But that would be cheating,' Julia said. 'I ought to find them myself.'

Arrow nodded, enjoying scrabbling at the damp sand with his fluffy front paws.

Golden sunshine glimmered on the waves and the breakers made a lovely shushing sound as they met the shore.

'I like the sea!' Arrow declared.

'Me too!' Julia said warmly, feeling a stir of affection for him. She was enjoying herself too. Having her magic bunny on holiday with her was the best fun ever.

Julia was digging in the sand with the toe of her trainer when she uncovered the tip of something buried. She bent down to finish digging it out with her hands.

'Wow! Look at this!' she cried, holding up an enormous shell.

It filled the palm of one hand. Even covered with damp sand it was impressive, with a spiral curve and lots of little spikes and ridges. Julia went to rinse it in the sea and then dried it on her T-shirt.

'This should earn us a few team points!' she said delightedly as she rejoined Arrow.

'Oi! That's *my* shell!' called a mean, nasal voice.

Julia looked up to see some older kids, a girl and two boys, walking towards her.

The girl who had spoken looked about twelve. She was short with thick arms and legs and wore a pair of baggy combat shorts.

She held out a meaty hand. 'Hand it over!'

Chapter
FIVE

Julia froze. 'This . . . erm . . . shell's mine.
I–I just found it,' she stammered.

The girl grinned nastily. 'Tough!'

'I'd do what Kelly says, if I were you,'
the dark-haired boy said.

'Yeah, you don't want to get on the
wrong side of her!' said the other boy. He
had curly hair and wore glasses.

'You heard Hitesh and Dean! Gimme

it!' Kelly ordered, lunging towards Julia and grabbing the shell.

Julia felt a warm tingling sensation down her spine and saw Arrow's key flash and a spurt of crystal mist appear.

She hid a grin. Big mistake, Kelly!

The invisible crystal mist surrounded the girl just as she snatched the shell away. Suddenly, Kelly shot backwards and landed on her behind just as a wave was

coming in. Sandy water shot everywhere, splashing over Hitesh and Dean.

Kelly threw Julia's shell up in the air as she fell. It whizzed straight back towards Julia. She caught it neatly and slipped it into her bag.

Kelly struggled to her feet, fists clenched. Her face was scarlet.

'Get her!' she yelled.

Julia had already bent down and scooped Arrow securely under one arm. She raced back along the beach towards her team-mates and teachers.

Hitesh and Dean ran after her, while Kelly plodded along behind them, still soaking wet from landing in the water.

Julia's trainers dug into the sand. Her legs ached with the effort of running, but she was almost there now.

Just before she reached the others, the three mean kids gave up. They turned and walked away.

'Thanks, Arrow. You were brilliant!' Julia puffed. 'I'd have hated to lose that shell.'

His bobtail twitched. 'I am glad I could help.'

Julia flopped down near the other Wolverines and took the shell out of her bag to dry in the sun.

'Whoa! That's a corker! Wait until Old Potty sees what we've found.' Lex had spotted her shell and quickly scooped it up. Before Julia could say anything, he had hurried off to show the teachers who were standing at the water's edge.

Julia smiled. Trust Lex to take the credit for her efforts! 'He just doesn't get what

team work means, does he!' she whispered to Arrow, slowly shaking her head.

'But we are a good team.' The magic bunny jumped into her lap and Julia stroked his soft silver-blue fur.

'We're the best,' she said fondly.

Everyone returned to camp for lunch. It was the Elks' turn to make the meal.

When it was ready, Julia and the other
Wolverines took their picnic back to their
tent. The sun and the breeze had dried
Julia's sleeping bag and all the wet clothes.
Two of her team-mates helped her gather
up the stuff, but they left the clothes airer
up and used it to dry their towels from
the beach.

'I'm going to sit in the sun for a few
minutes to get warm,' Julia said to her
team-mates, shivering for effect. 'Back in
a minute.' She walked a little way down
the camping field and sat on the grass, so
she could share her cheese-salad sandwich
and apple with Arrow. The magic bunny
nibbled a lettuce leaf as he stretched
out beside her, enjoying the warmth on
his fur.

'I wonder what's going on over there?'

Julia glanced into the next field. Another group of children had just arrived and were unloading bags and camping equipment. 'Looks like another school's setting up next door.'

She watched the new kids choosing their pitches. Some boys and girls came towards the dividing fence, just a few metres away from where Julia and Arrow sat.

'Oh no!' Julia almost choked on her sandwich as she recognized a familiar squat shape, wearing combat shorts with a big sandy stain on the seat ...

It was Kelly! And Hitesh and Dean were with her.

Kelly spotted Julia and sauntered over towards the fence. She had a nasty smile on her broad face.

'If it isn't that snotty kid from the beach,' she sneered, resting her arms on the fence rail. Dean and Hitesh came to stand beside her. 'No one makes a fool of me and gets away with it. That's a promise.'

Julia's tummy fluttered with nerves. Kelly seemed even meaner than she remembered. And with Dean and Hitesh, the trio made a menacing sight. She gulped, not knowing what to say.

'Who are those kids?' Lex asked, walking up to Julia. He was flapping his damp beach towel about like a flag.

'I met them on the beach. They tried to pinch that big shell I found,' Julia told him quietly.

'Oh they did, did they?' Lex said loudly. He glared across the fence.

'What's it got to do with you anyway?'
Kelly jabbed a finger at him. 'I'd stay out
of it, if I were you,' she warned.

'You heard Kelly,' said Dean. 'We're
known as the Rockets at our school. You
don't wanna mess with us!'

'So what? We're the Wolverines,' Lex
said, unimpressed.

'Funny, cos you look like a bunch of wimps to me!' Kelly said. 'You should be called the Tadpoles or something!'

Dean and Hitesh sniggered. 'That told 'em, Kel!' Hitesh said.

Kelly smirked. She turned her back and walked away. The two boys followed her.

Lex leaned over the fence. 'Yeah? Well – you lot are just hot air! So you should be called the Balloons!' he shouted after them.

Julia's tummy still felt all fluttery. She was grateful to Lex for sticking up for her, but she wasn't convinced that joining in the name-calling had been a good idea.

'That Kelly girl seems like the type to hold a grudge,' she whispered to Arrow, while Lex went to hang up his towel to dry.

The bunny nodded, his whiskers twitching worriedly. 'I think so too.'

Julia hoped she was wrong, but she had a horrible feeling that Lex had just made things ten times worse.

Chapter
SIX

'What's the difference between an elephant and a biscuit?' Julia asked, the following evening after supper. Everyone was gathered in the common room.

'Go on then,' Lex rolled his eyes. 'What's the difference between an elephant and a biscuit?'

'You can't dunk an elephant in your tea!' Julia said triumphantly.

'That's a terrible joke!' Ellie groaned,
but she laughed.

Lex and the other Wolverines joined in.

Arrow was in Julia's bag. One of his
little silver-blue ears swivelled sideways
with puzzlement.

'What is an elephant?'

'It's a really big animal with a long
nose, called a trunk,' Julia answered in
a whisper.

'I do not understand why that is funny.'

'It's not. Elephants are amazing. It's the elephant *joke* that's funny!' Julia reassured him. Her team-mates were a bit close to risk a long explanation. She bit back a smile as she wondered whether Arrow and the other magic rabbits told each other silly jokes.

It had been a fun day with all the teams learning more about farm work. They had stood by while the farmer whistled instructions to his three black-and-white border collies as they rounded up the sheep. Even Ellie hadn't complained when they'd had to walk across the muddy fields to watch. Afterwards they had watched a video about lambing and then had a quiz, which the Bears had won.

'Those sheep dogs were brilliant earlier, weren't they?' Julia said softly to Arrow.

'Yes,' he agreed, but then gave a tiny shudder. 'But I would not want to get too close to them.'

'No, of course not.' Julia slipped her hand into her bag to stroke him reassuringly. Her cute friend was so little and the collies must have seemed very large and scary to him. 'Don't worry. I'll keep you safe.'

'Thank you. You are a good friend.' Arrow rubbed his velvety cheek against her fingers.

The Cougars and the Bears started a table-tennis match on the other side of the common room, and the rest of the Wolverines went to watch. As the ball pinged back and forth, Julia found her thoughts turning to Kelly, Dean and Hitesh. Despite her worries nothing else had happened. The previous night had passed without incident and the neighbouring field had been empty all that day, as the older school kids had gone on a day trip.

Then Julia heard voices and laughter in the yard. The other school were back from their trip. She tensed, and hoped she could avoid coming face to face with the tough girl and her mates.

But Kelly, Hitesh and Dean did not appear when some of the older kids came into the common room. Julia felt herself relaxing.

'Maybe we're worrying about nothing,' she whispered to Arrow.

He nodded. 'I hope so.'

Julia moved away from the table-tennis game and went over to the small old-fashioned TV, which was showing a wildlife programme about meerkats. She found an empty chair and sat with Arrow on her lap. It had been a long day and she soon felt her eyelids drooping as the programme ended.

'All right everyone. Time to turn in,' Mr Potter said. 'Don't forget, Wolverines, you're doing the cooking tomorrow. So you have an extra early start.'

'OK, sir.' Julia stifled a yawn as she rose to her feet.

Later, as Julia snuggled up with Arrow in her cosy sleeping bag, a feeling of contentment crept over her. It really felt like everyone was part of a team now, especially as Lex and Ellie seemed to be trying to get on a bit better. She couldn't wait to find out what the teachers had planned for them tomorrow.

Julia was in the middle of a lovely dream about visiting Moonglow Meadow and meeting all of Arrow's magical rabbit friends, when she woke abruptly. She sat upright, staring into the semi-darkness. Her ears strained to make out the faint rustling sounds that had broken into her dream.

Beside her, Arrow stirred and stretched his back legs.

'Did you hear that? There's something outside,' Julia whispered, her heart pounding.

Her magic bunny stiffened. 'My enemies have found me!'

Before Julia could stop him, Arrow had scrabbled out of the sleeping bag and leapt for the half-unzipped porch door. But the zip held and Arrow's fluffy little body got stuck halfway through.

As her tiny friend wriggled and squirmed in panic, Julia heard a familiar nasal voice.

'Cut the guy ropes, so the tent collapses on those dumb kids!' Kelly ordered.

There were muffled titters.

'Yeah! That'll teach them to call us

names!' said a boy's voice.

Arrow was still struggling to escape.
He seemed terrified. Squirming out of
her sleeping bag, Julia leaned forward and
gently grasped Arrow round his furry
middle.

'Arrow! Wait!' she whispered urgently.
'It's not dark rabbits out there. Listen. It's
those mean kids!'

Arrow pricked his ears and then
gradually stopped struggling. Julia was
able to jiggle the zip open so she could
free him and pull him gently towards her.
She held her friend close, dismayed at
how fast his little heart was beating.

'It's OK. You're safe with me,' she
crooned. She felt her temper rising on
Arrow's behalf. How dare those bullies
scare her friend? 'I'm going out there to

see what those silly idiots are doing!' she stormed.

Arrow's eyes twinkled. 'No. I have a better idea!'

Julia felt a familiar warm prickling sensation down her back as Arrow's key flashed and a cloud of sparkling crystal mist appeared and whirled around her and Arrow as if they were inside a snow globe. Something very strange was about to happen.

Chapter
SEVEN

The sparkling crystal mist floated towards
the unzipped porch door and disappeared
outside the tent.

'What have you done?' Julia asked
Arrow curiously.

The magic bunny pricked his ears.
'Come and see!'

He hopped forward and Julia crept
after him towards the entrance to the tent.

Carefully lifting the flap, she crouched there with Arrow and peeped outside.

Her mouth opened in surprise as she saw the sparkling dust sink into the beach towels her team had left to dry on the airer. All of a sudden, the towels rose silently into the air and began flapping towards Kelly and her gang like giant multicoloured bats.

'That's brilliant, Arrow!' Julia whispered. She held her hands pressed to her mouth to hold in her delighted laughter. Kelly, Dean and Hitesh hadn't noticed the beach towels yet. But they were going to see them any minute now.

Julia began counting silently. One. Two. Three!

'Argh!' Kelly yelled, staggering backwards and waving her arms about. 'I'm being attacked! Get 'em off!'

One of the towels flopped on to Hitesh's head. He almost tripped over his own feet as he spun round and threw it off. 'This field's haunted!'

'Leg it!' cried Dean, ducking as a bright orange towel with a blue dolphin pattern flapped around him.

Kelly dived for the fence. She

clambered over and there was a thud as she landed in a heap. Muffled cries rose as the others fell on top of her.

'Ow! Get off me, you morons!' Kelly hissed.

The arguing voices faded as the older kids dashed for their tent and disappeared inside it. Julia was still trying not to laugh out loud. She looked down at Arrow who sat beside her.

His rainbow-bright brown eyes twinkled up at her. 'I do not think they will be back tonight!'

His key started glowing again and there was a bright flash. The towels stopped floating about in mid-air and drifted gently back to the airer.

Still giggling silently at what had just happened, Julia crept back into the tent.

Astonishingly, the other Wolverines were still fast asleep and had missed all the excitement.

'Thanks, Arrow. You can do such amazing things,' Julia whispered, stroking his warm fur.

Her magic bunny reached round to nuzzle her hand. 'You helped me, when I thought my enemies were close. So I am glad I could help you,' he said.

Something occurred to Julia. 'What if it really *had* been dark rabbits outside? Would you have had to go back to Moonglow Meadow?' she asked anxiously.

Arrow nodded. 'I am afraid I would,' he told her gently. 'I must always protect the key. It is my duty as guardian.'

'Well, now you don't need to leave. Maybe you could stay with me forever? I could help you keep the key safe,' Julia said hopefully.

'I am sorry. That is not possible,' Arrow said gently. 'I will stay until Moonglow Meadow urgently needs more magic. When that happens, I may have to leave at once, without saying goodbye. Do you understand, Julia?'

Julia nodded, trying not to get upset, and she decided to enjoy every moment of their time together, however long that might be.

'I hate wobbly bacon. I want mine cooked more than that!' Ellie fussed, looking over Lex's shoulder.

Lex stepped back from the cooker. 'Well, you do it then! I'll stir the beans instead. Unless you've got a problem with them too?'

Ellie banged the frying pan about as she turned the rashers. 'No, but just stay out of my way, OK?'

'Me? You're getting in *my* way!'

Julia hid a groan. Ellie and Lex were at it again. And they'd been getting on so well the day before. She had a funny feeling that they liked each other though, even if they did argue.

'I'm just glad I'm in charge of the toaster!' she said to Arrow.

He sat invisibly on the work surface, watching her in fascination. *Ping!* Another two slices of toasted bread popped up. Julia lifted them out and put two more slices of bread in, before adding the toast to the pile on a plate.

'I like toast!' Arrow licked his lips, his nose twitching.

Despite the squabbling, breakfast was

cooked on time. Julia and the rest of the Wolverines served the other teams and then finally sat down as well.

Mr Potter and the other teachers sat nearby.

'. . . strange rumours about haunted towels, if you please!' Mr Potter was saying. 'I heard a teacher from the other school talking about it in the shower block.'

'Moonlight *can* play very strange tricks,' Miss Granger laughed. She was one of Julia's favourite teachers.

They all laughed. Julia did too. She glanced down at Arrow who sat on her lap. No one would ever believe what had really happened!

After breakfast, the Elks washed up and cleared away and then everyone had

a game of cricket in the camping field.
Next door, the older school kids were
being shown how to make a temporary
shelter from what they could find lying
about in the woods.

Julia noticed Kelly looking her way as
she dragged a branch back across the field.
There was a thoughtful expression on
the girl's spiteful face. *Maybe she still hasn't
learned that it's a bad idea to pick on younger
kids – especially with Arrow around*, Julia
thought.

In the afternoon, the teams were
allowed to walk with a teacher into the
nearby village. Arrow had curled his front
paws over the opening of Julia's backpack
and was enjoying the scenery.

When they arrived in the village, to
Julia's disappointment most of the shops

were closed. She had hoped to buy her magic bunny a treat with her pocket money. She and Arrow were passing a charity shop when something in the window caught her eye.

'Wow! Look at those cool roller boots!' Julia enthused. 'That tag next to them says

they're my size too. My old boots are too small for me now. I've wanted some new ones for ages and I've just got enough money to buy these. What a shame the shop's closed.'

'I could get them for you with my magic,' Arrow offered. 'You could put the money through the door.'

Julia was tempted, but she shook her head. 'Better not. They would be difficult to hide. Miss Granger would notice and ask loads of questions. Maybe we could come back for them another time.'

Arrow nodded. 'Very well.'

'Thanks anyway for wanting to help.' Julia smiled fondly at her friend. She checked the shop's opening times. 'It's open again on Thursday.'

She glanced at the window one last

time before she and Arrow moved away.
The roller boots were white with red stars
on the ankles and red laces. She could
already imagine herself zooming down
the street on them.

Chapter
EIGHT

Thursday dawned bright and clear.

The week seemed to have sped by and Julia could hardly believe that this was the last full day of the holiday. Early next morning they'd all be going home. She felt a bit sad about leaving. Ellie and Lex had certainly made the holiday more interesting – they were finally getting on better now, making jokes and being more friendly towards each other.

'I can't stop thinking about those roller boots,' she said to Arrow. 'I hope there'll be time to go back to the shop in the village.'

Arrow nodded.

But the entire morning was taken up with a cross-country hike. Everyone, including Julia, arrived back at camp tired and hungry. It was the Bears' turn to make lunch and they soon turned out mounds of delicious egg sandwiches and fresh lemonade.

'I hope you've all recovered,' Mr Potter said, as Julia and Arrow sprawled on the grass afterwards with all the other kids, enjoying the warm sunshine. 'Miss Granger has organized a treasure hunt.'

'That's right.' Miss Granger handed out

printed sheets of paper. 'I've made a list of things for you to find. You'll win points for everything you bring back to camp.'

The teams huddled in groups as they studied the lists.

'This will be fun,' Julia told Arrow as they set off. 'You can join in and help me look for stuff.'

Arrow pricked up his floppy ears. 'I would like that.'

'OK. Ready troops?' Mr Potter sent the Bears and Cougars off in one direction, and the Wolverines and Elks in another.

It was a lovely afternoon and Julia enjoyed wandering slowly across the fields with Arrow hopping along beside her. Now and then he stopped to nibble a patch of clover or snuffle a wild flower.

As they reached the woods, Julia and her team-mates went off in different directions to find the items they'd decided to look for.

'We have to find a fir cone,' she told Arrow, as everyone spread out under the trees.

The silver-blue bunny reared up on to his back legs excitedly. 'I know of these from my world! Pine nuts are delicious!' he told her eagerly.

Leaping forward he began snuffling around in the leaves that lined the forest floor and then dived beneath a clump of fern. The tall fronds waggled about as Arrow rooted beneath them. After a few seconds he backed out of the ferns, dragging the most enormous fir cone Julia had ever seen. It was almost as big as his whole body.

She only just managed not to burst out laughing. Her friend's furry little sides heaved as he dropped the fir cone at her feet.

'Well done! Thanks, Arrow.'

'You are welcome,' he puffed proudly, looking pleased with himself.

Holding the fir cone, and with Arrow tucked invisibly under one arm, Julia joined the other Wolverines. Between them, they had found most things on the list.

Lex had found an oak leaf. He twirled

it between his fingers as he stood looking down at Ellie who was on her knees, her fingers combing through the grass. 'All we need now is a pink flower petal,' he said to her.

'There are plenty of yellow flowers and here's a blue one,' Ellie murmured. 'I've been looking for ages, but pink ones are difficult to find.'

'Well, look harder,' Lex suggested.

'I am!' Ellie said crossly. 'I don't see you looking. You could help, instead of just standing there giving orders!'

Lex sighed heavily. 'I've found an oak leaf, haven't I? Come on, hurry up. We don't want to be the last ones back.'

Julia looked meaningfully at Arrow. Lex was being so bossy, even though Ellie was trying really hard.

'I'll help you,' Julia said, scanning the ground with Ellie.

It took ages to find a pink flower and it was Arrow who eventually sniffed one out. Julia whispered her thanks as she carefully picked one petal. 'Yay! That's it! We've finished,' she called in a louder voice.

'Thanks, Julia,' Ellie said, smiling.

'Yeah. And sorry for being a grouch,' Lex murmured, giving Ellie a friendly shove. Grinning, she shoved him back.

The Wolverines returned triumphantly to camp, to find the Elks and Cougars already there. The Bears arrived shortly after and everyone spread out their treasures.

Mr Potter and Miss Granger awarded team points and then everyone crowded round the wall chart to watch as she added them up to find out the final scores.

'A dead heat!' Mr Potter declared, with a rare smile. 'Well done everyone.'

'Yay!' It was a popular result. Bears, Wolverines, Elks and Cougars whooped and capered about, exchanging high fives.

'We'll have a barbeque this evening to celebrate our last night,' Miss Granger announced. Ellie looked excitedly at

Julia and Lex gave her thumbs up. Julia grinned back at them both, proud of the Wolverines' teamwork.

It was only later, when everyone was busy in the farmyard organizing the barbeque, that Julia suddenly remembered that she wanted to go to the village.

'Oh no! It's my last chance to buy those roller boots before we go home,' she said, disappointedly. 'Maybe we could run over there now? If we hurry, we can be back in camp before anyone notices.'

Arrow's eyes were troubled. 'Are you sure, Julia? Will you get into trouble?'

Julia chewed her lip. She knew the rules about going off alone. But she wouldn't *be* alone. She'd be with Arrow and he had his magic to protect them.

But she knew that Mr Potter and the

other teachers wouldn't see it that way.

'I'll leave a note on my sleeping bag, just to be on the safe side,' she told her magic bunny. 'That way, they'll know where I am. Although we'll be back long before anyone finds it.'

It took about ten minutes or so of doing old-fashioned Scouts' pace to reach the village outskirts. 'Twenty running paces, twenty walking,' Julia puffed, swinging her arms. 'Gran told me she learned this in the Girl Guides.'

She was breathing hard by the time they headed into the village. The charity shop was directly ahead of them. Julia frowned as they drew closer. There didn't seem to be any lights on in the shop.

'Oh no! It must have closed early!'

The roller boots were still on display behind the glass pane. They were so close, but they might as well have been on the moon.

'I am sorry. We were too late.' Arrow's fluffy silver-blue ears drooped sadly.

'It wasn't your fault.' Julia swallowed her disappointment. She really would have loved those roller boots. 'Oh well,'

she sighed. 'It's just one of those things.'

Julia lifted Arrow out of her bag and stroked his warm soft fur that smelled of grass and sunshine.

'Having you for my friend is better than anything though. Even new roller boots.'

All of a sudden, three familiar figures emerged from a nearby alley. As Julia spotted them, her tummy clenched. Kelly, Dean and Hitesh saw her too and began walking towards her.

'Uh-oh,' Julia breathed nervously.

'It's that dozy kid again,' Dean cried, shoving his glasses more firmly on to his nose.

'Watch out. Weird things happen around her,' Hitesh warned.

'Hey! What are you doin' with that

bunny?' Kelly shouted at Julia.

Julia gasped. They could *see* Arrow!

Her tiny friend must have thought it was safe to remain visible as they were so far from the campsite. Now that the mean kids had spotted him, Arrow couldn't use his magic without giving himself away.

'He . . . mine,' Julia said shakily, holding Arrow protectively.

Kelly's pudgy face creased in a grin. 'Yeah! Well he's not any more. Give him to me. Or else!'

Chapter
NINE

Julia couldn't move. Her knees seemed to have turned to jelly. The three older kids had spread out across the pavement, blocking her way.

What was she going to do?

'Cute bunny. I think I'll call him Fluffy.' Kelly's eyes gleamed. She reached out and her fingers brushed Arrow's soft fur.

He flinched and gave a tiny whimper.

Julia was jolted into action. Whirling round, she ran as fast as she could.

'Oi! Come back with Fluffy!' Kelly yelled.

The bullies gave chase. Julia could hear their feet pounding behind her.

She was a fast runner, even holding Arrow. But she was already puffed out from jogging across the fields to get here and she only had a small head-start.

Worse still, she realized she was running the wrong way. The campsite was in the opposite direction!

'They're gaining on us!' Julia panted, trying to ignore the stitch in her side.

'Turn down this side street, Julia,' Arrow instructed.

Julia did, but then her heart almost missed a beat. 'It's a dead end!'

Kelly and her mates were out of sight, but they'd be here any second.

Arrow's key flashed and Julia felt a familiar tingling down her spine as a whoosh of crystal mist appeared and whirled round her feet before disappearing.

Whirr! Rumble! Slide! Well-oiled wheels shot smoothly across the pavement.

Wheels? She glanced down to see that she was wearing roller boots! White ones with red stars on the ankles and red laces.

Julia zoomed forward with an amazing fresh burst of speed. She felt happiness shining through her. It felt fantastic to be skating along the smooth road.

'There!' Arrow pointed one tiny paw at a narrow gap between two houses. It wasn't a dead end after all!

Julia checked her stride. Shifting her weight, she skidded into an expert turn and skated down the narrow path. After weaving down alleys and side roads, she emerged halfway down the main road almost back at the charity shop.

She had managed to double-back on herself, and was now racing in the direction of the campsite.

'Those bullies will never catch us now!' she said, grinning. She could imagine their puzzled faces as they tried to work out where she and Arrow had gone!

Julia slowed down just long enough to gently put her magic bunny into her backpack, where he hunched next to the trainers she'd been wearing earlier. He'd thought of everything!

'Yay! These boots are amazing!' Julia felt the breeze whistling past her and stirring her wavy hair. She bent forward slightly, pumping her arms for balance and extra speed.

'You are a very good skater. You could keep the boots.' Arrow's whiskers twitched mischievously as he poked his head out of her bag.

'Really? Do you think I could?' Julia

said eagerly. 'But . . .'

She had a brainwave. They were approaching the charity shop. She stopped just long enough to fish some money out of her jeans pocket. She thrust it through the shop's letterbox, where the shop assistant would find it the next morning.

'There. All done! You're the best friend in the whole world, Arrow!'

Julia and Arrow reached the path across the fields in record time. There was still no sign of Kelly and her mates so Julia quickly changed back into her trainers, leapt over the stile and dived into the tent. She stuffed the roller boots into her bag with her other clothes.

Julia emerged from the tent with Arrow in her backpack. They started to walk up the field towards the farmyard. The smell of sizzling sausages and beef burgers wafted towards her, making Julia's tummy rumble. She couldn't wait to get to the barbeque.

She half expected Old Potty to storm towards her, demanding to know where she'd been, but nothing happened.

'I think we've got away with it,' Julia was saying, when there was a shout from behind her. Glancing over her shoulder, she spotted Kelly, Hitesh and Dean. They were just clambering over the stile.

'Oh no!' Julia quickened her steps towards the farm, but then she noticed Arrow's key glowing more brightly than she had ever seen it.

He leapt out of her bag and ran behind the nearest tent, his white bobtail flashing.

Julia knew that the moment she had been dreading was here. Without a second thought for the older kids who were chasing her, she ran after him.

As she rounded the tent, she saw that her fluffy little friend had gone. Arrow stood there in his true form. A tiny cute silver-blue bunny no longer, but a magnificent rabbit the size of a large cat. His silky pure white fur was flecked with silver and his large upright ears had glittering silver tips.

'Arrow!' Julia gasped, amazed all over again by his beauty. 'Are you leaving right now?'

Arrow's eyes softened and jewel-bright rainbows gleamed in them. 'I must. Moonglow Meadow urgently needs more of the key's magic.'

Julia's chest tightened with sadness. She
bit back tears because she knew she must
be brave and let her friend go. Bending
down, she threw her arms around the
majestic white rabbit and laid her cheek
against his silky fur.

'I'll never forget you,' she whispered,
her voice breaking.

'Nor I you. You have been a good friend.' Arrow allowed her to hug him for a moment longer and then gently moved back. 'Farewell. Always follow your dreams, Julia,' he said in a smooth velvety voice.

There was a final flash from his key and crystal dust drifted down around Julia, crackling like sparks from dying fireworks as it hit the grass. Arrow was gone.

Julia stood there; hardly able to believe how fast everything had happened. A tear rolled down her cheek. Something lay on the grass. It was a crystal rainbow drop. She picked it up and it tingled against her palm as it turned into a pure white pebble in the shape of a bunny.

Julia slipped it into her pocket. She knew she would keep it forever as a reminder of the wonderful adventure she had shared with her magic bunny.

Sadly, she walked slowly out from behind the tent – smack into Kelly and her mates.

Kelly stood in front of her. 'Thought you could hide, did ya?'

Julia gulped. She dashed away a tear and prepared to face the bullies.

'Hey!' called a voice behind her. 'Leave her alone!'

Julia turned to see Lex running down the field. Ellie was with him and two more of her team-mates weren't far behind.

'You pick on one of the Wolverines, you pick on all of us!' Lex said.

'Yeah!' Ellie had a fierce look on her face. 'That goes for me too! We're a team!'

Julia turned to look at Lex and Ellie, who were both standing with their hands on their hips. It seemed that Arrow wasn't the only friend she'd made this holiday. Her fear evaporated as she stood facing the bullies alongside her team-mates.

Kelly's face paled. She obviously didn't like being outnumbered. 'Come on. They're not worth it,' she murmured. The three bullies slunk away towards their own camp.

'And don't try that again, or else!' Lex called after them. His team-mates whooped agreement.

'Where've you been? We've been looking for you,' Ellie said more quietly to Julia.

'I just wanted to be by myself for a little while,' Julia said.

Ellie smiled sympathetically. 'I know. I'm a bit sad about leaving too. I love our team. It's been a fab holiday, hasn't it?'

'The best one ever!'

'I . . . um . . . I know I can be a bit of a pain sometimes,' Ellie began, blushing. 'But I was wondering if you, me and Lucy might do some stuff together when we get home? You two always seem to have fun, but I . . . I didn't like to butt in.'

Julia grinned. 'You wouldn't be butting in. We'd love it!' She gave Ellie a quick hug and Ellie beamed at her as she returned it.

'And this holiday's not over yet!' Julia felt a smile spreading over her face. 'Come on, Wolverines!' she cried, heading for the barbeque in the farmyard with her team-mates.

Wherever Arrow was, she knew that he'd be smiling too. *Take care. And say hi from me to all your friends in Moonglow Meadow,* she whispered under her breath.

Win a Magic Bunny goody bag!

Strike, the leader of the bunnies of Moonglow Meadow,
has an urgent message for Arrow that will keep him safe from the
dark rabbits who are trying to capture the magic key.

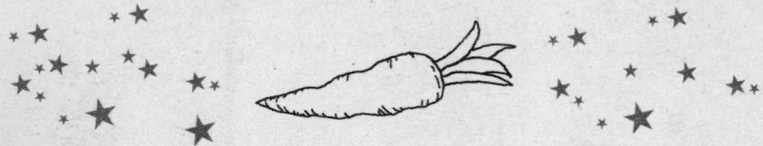

Three words from the message can be found in the special carrots that
are hidden in *Classroom Capers* and *A Splash of Magic*. Find the hidden
words and put them together to complete Strike's message.
Send it in to us and each month we will put every correct message
in a draw and pick out one lucky winner who will
receive a special Magic Bunny prize.

Send your secret message, name and address on a postcard to:
Magic Bunny competition
Puffin Books
80 Strand
London WC2R 0RL

Hurry, Arrow needs your help!

Good luck!

puffin.co.uk

Look Out For

Chocolate Wishes
9780141332413

Holiday Dreams*
9780141332420

Dancing Days
9780141332437

Classroom Capers
9780141332444

A Splash of Magic
9780141332451

puffin.co.uk

It all started with a Scarecrow.

Puffin is seventy years old.
Sounds ancient, doesn't it? But Puffin has never been
so lively. We're always on the lookout for the next big
idea, which is how it began all those years ago.

Penguin Books was a big idea from the mind of
a man called Allen Lane, who in 1935 invented
the quality paperback and changed the world.
**And from great Penguins, great Puffins grew,
changing the face of children's books forever.**

The first four Puffin Picture Books were hatched in 1940 and the
first Puffin story book featured a man with broomstick arms called
Worzel Gummidge. In 1967 Kaye Webb, Puffin Editor, started the
Puffin Club, promising to **'make children into readers'**.
She kept that promise and over 200,000 children became
devoted Puffineers through their quarterly instalments of
Puffin Post, which is now back for a new generation.

Many years from now, we hope you'll look back and
remember Puffin with a smile. **No matter what your age
or what you're into, there's a Puffin for everyone.**
The possibilities are endless, but one thing is for sure:
whether it's a picture book or a paperback, a sticker book
or a hardback, **if it's got that little Puffin
on it – it's bound to be good.**